Tad Meets The GRUMBLY GRUMBLEBEE

By John Fornof

Ribbits! is a creation of Bob Garner

Illustrated by Bernard Adnet

Do everything without complaining or arguing.
Philippians 2:14 NIV

Zonderkidz

Zonder**kidz**®

The children's group of Zondervan

www.zonderkidz.com

Tad Meets The Grumbly Grumblebee
Copyright © 2004 by Focus on the Family
Based on a concept by Bob Garner
ISBN: 0-310-70716-1

Requests for information should be addressed to:
Zonderkidz, Grand Rapids, Michigan 49530

Editor: Barbara J. Scott
Interior Design & Art Direction: Laura M. Maitner

Printed in Singapore
04 05 06 07/TP/4 3 2 1

Tad sat on a great big toadstool and sighed a great big sigh. He thought about all the chores he had to do. He thought about all the homework he had to do.

"Why do I have to do all this work?" he said out loud. "All my friends get to play today. Why not me?"

I know exactly how you feel," said a wee voice. Tad looked around. He didn't see anyone.

"Down here, buddy," said the voice.

Tad looked down and spotted a plump little bumblebee, wearing a little purple hat.

"The name's Grumblebee."

"I'm Tad. It's nice to meet you."

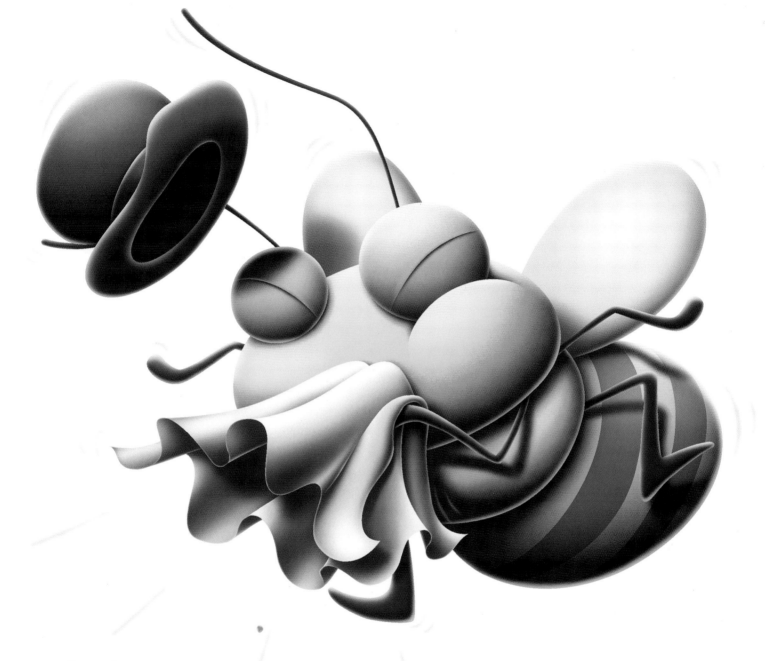

"Yeah, I'm sure it is. Look, kid, you don't have it half as bad as I do. I buzz these flowers 'round here every day from dawn to dusk. And what do I get? Yucky yellow pollen dust all over my legs. Did I tell you I'm allergic to pollen? Makes me break out in hives."

Tad had some grumbles of his own. "Well, *I* have to take out the garbage *and* wash the dishes *and* straighten my room *and* do my homework *and* study for my spelling test."

They grumbled back and forth so much,
Tad didn't have time to finish his work.

When he finally came inside, his dad had some bad news.
"I'm sorry, Son, but you can't go to the ball game with me
tonight. You didn't finish your homework, and you didn't finish
your chores."

Tad sighed a great big sigh. "This is so unfair!"

"I know exactly how you feel," said a wee voice. The Grumblebee was back!

"All of us bees do all the work-work-work, while our Queeny Bee sits there on her royal throne. Did I tell you we're talkin' about goin' on strike? At least that's the buzz around the hive."

Tad and The Grumblebee grumbled so long, Tad got to bed late. He woke up grumpy and grumbly the next morning.

While walking to school, Tad heard a tiny whistle. He looked down to see a little stinkbug digging a hole in the ground.

"Hi there," said the bug. "I'm The Happy Stinkbug. Uh, you aren't going to eat me, are you?"

"No," said Tad. "Stinkbugs give me bad breath."

"Wonderful!" said The Happy Stinkbug. "Say, isn't this a great day?"

"No," Tad grumbled. "Why?"

"For one, you aren't going to eat me. And for that, I'm very thankful. But I'm also thankful for the beautiful breeze and the fluffy white clouds and the way the birds are singing this morning."

"I didn't notice," Tad said. "I guess I was too busy grumbling."

"I used to grumble about everything, too," said The Happy Stinkbug. "In fact, I was called The *Grumpy* Stinkbug. And I felt really rotten. Then I read the Great Book, where it says 'be thankful.' I tried it. And you know what? It makes a big difference in my day!"

That afternoon, Tad took out the garbage, washed the dishes, straightened his room, did his homework, and studied for his spelling test. He *tried* to be thankful.

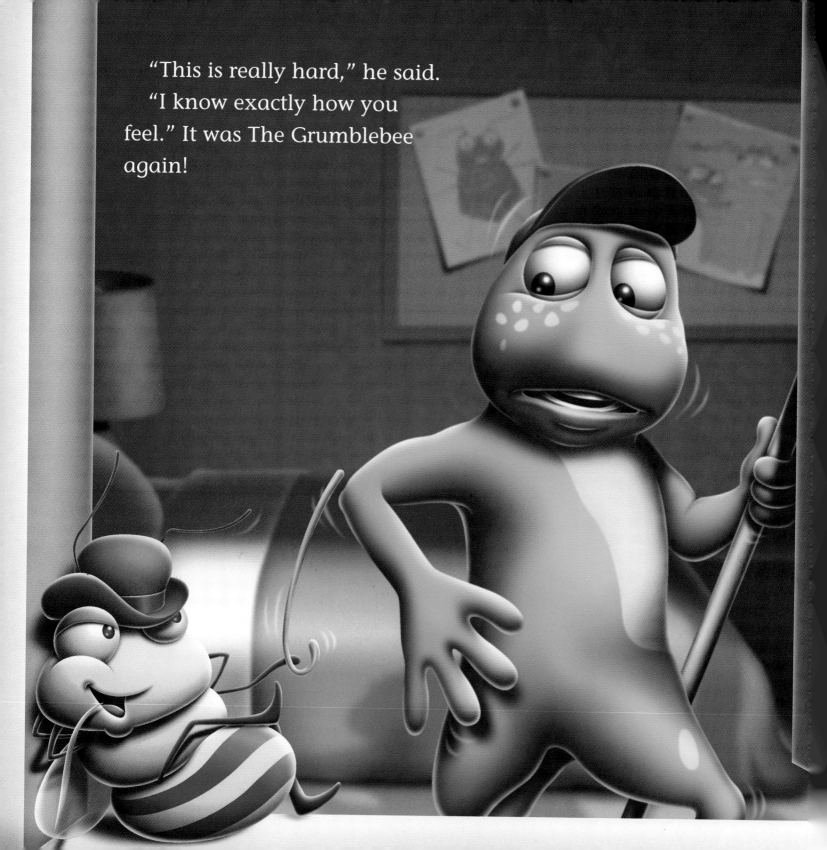

"This is really hard," he said. "I know exactly how you feel." It was The Grumblebee again!

Hmmm, Tad thought. *Every time The Grumblebee shows up, something bad happens. And I feel very grumpy.*

This time, Tad told The Grumblebee to buzz off. "Sorry, but I'm not going to listen to your grumbling anymore," Tad said. "Well suit yourself, kid," said The Grumblebee. And with that, he whirled around and buzzed away.

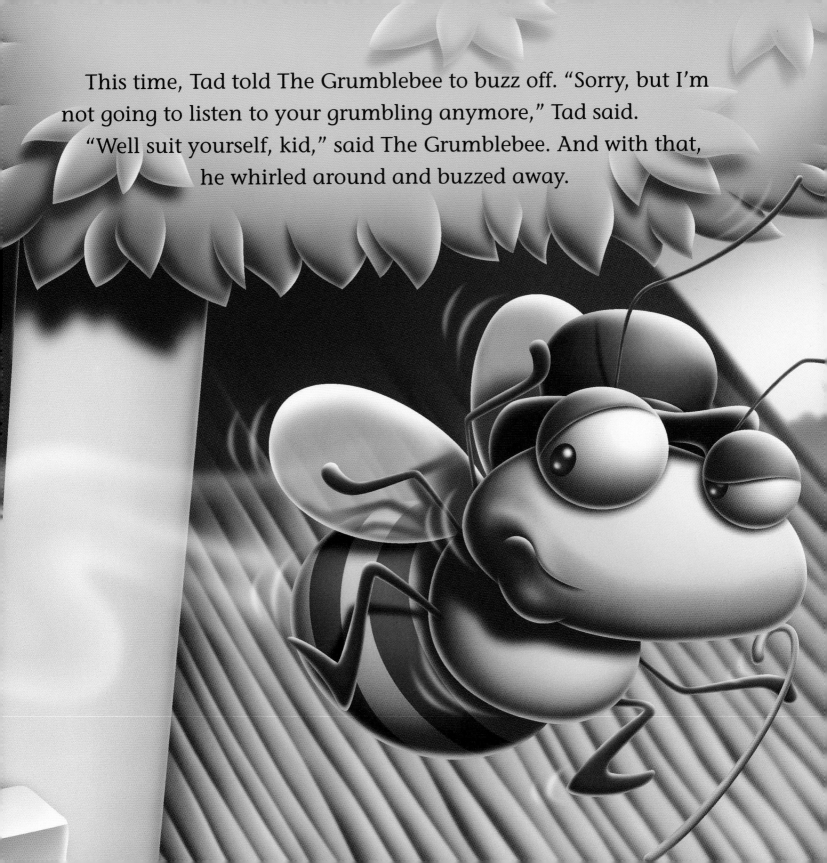

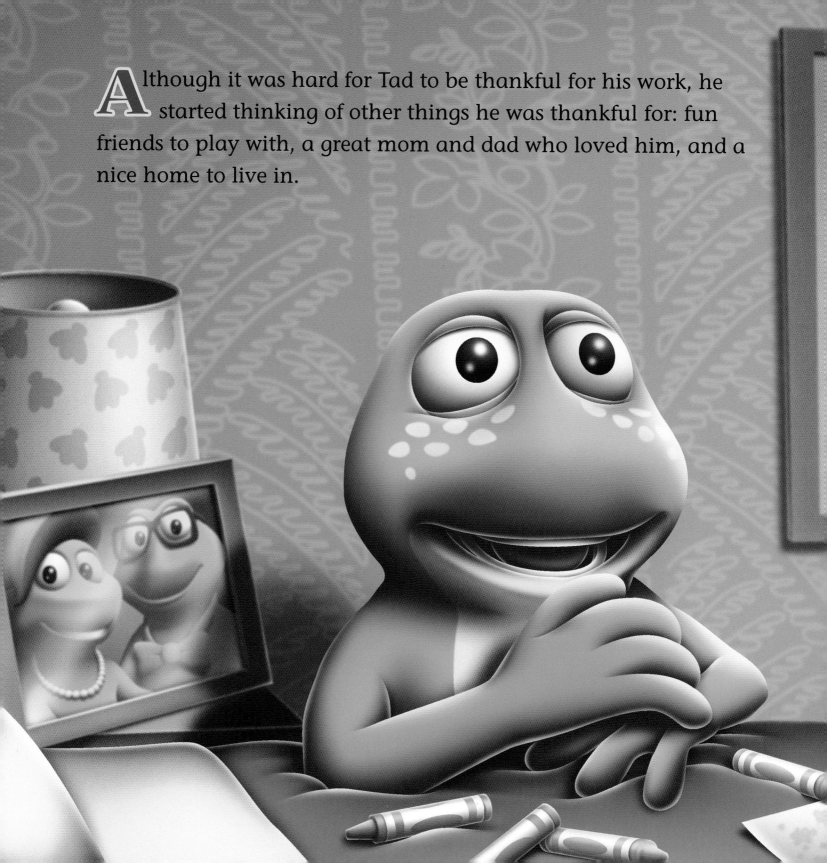

Although it was hard for Tad to be thankful for his work, he started thinking of other things he was thankful for: fun friends to play with, a great mom and dad who loved him, and a nice home to live in.

As he worked, his day seemed to go a little better. He started to whistle. And now, as he thought of all the things he was thankful for, he was most thankful he had met a little friend named The Happy Stinkbug.